No More Señora Mimí

*To the babysitters who make room in
their hearts and homes*

MM

*For Elinor, Ingrid, Lyndon,
Thea, and Gwen*

BC

No More Señora Mimí

MEG MEDINA

CANDLEWICK PRESS

ILLUSTRATED BY
BRITTANY CICCHESE

Señora Mimí lives upstairs in apartment 4C.
Every day Mami drops me off on her way to work.

Señora Mimí has a two-tooth baby named Nelson and a no-tooth dog named Pancho, who likes buttered crackers as much as I do.

"Please hurry, Ana," señora Mimí says this morning.
"You'll be late for school." She clips wiggly Nelson into
his stroller and searches everywhere for Pancho's leash.

I'm too excited to finish eating, so I slip my dish in the sink. Abuela is moving in with Mami and me tonight! The pink bedroom next to our kitchen will be hers. I've already put my best stuffed bear on the pillow to welcome her.

"From now on, Abuela will watch me while Mami is at work," I say. "She's staying forever."

"That's right," señora Mimí says. "Now anda, little one. We'll have to go corre-corre to get to school before the bell."

Señora Mimí puts on her sweater, the striped one like the one she made for me. She waits while I sing the shoelace song and tie my sneakers, rabbit ears and double knots, just the way she showed me.

"Vamos, Ana," she says. "We're almost out of time."

Outside, the wind blows as we hurry along the bumpy sidewalk.
I kick the leaves that swirl at my feet and notice a game of
hopscotch peeking out from under a crunchy pile. But when
I start to jump, señora Mimí calls me away.

"There's no time to play pon now," she says.

"I bet Abuela will let me stop and play whenever I want," I say.
My words make dragon puffs in the air between us.

But señora Mimí just waves good morning to Mrs. Curtis.
"Let's hold hands while we cross, Ana," she says.

Señora Mimí's cheeks are pink and her eyes are shiny from the cold when she hands me my lunch sack.

"Have a good day, Ana," she says. "See you after school!"

My class is already lined up to go inside.

"Abuela is coming to live with me!" I tell my teacher, Mrs. Kapoor, at the door. "She's going to take care of me from now on, so I won't need a babysitter."

"How exciting!" says Mrs. Kapoor. "A grandmother to see every day."

When it's my turn in the writing center, I make a list of all the fun things that my mejor del mundo abuela and I will do together. Then I share it in circle time.

"Lucky you!" Tynisha says. "Grandmothers are way better than bossy babysitters! No more señora Mimí to tell you what to do every day!"

"Oh," I say, startled. No more señora Mimí? I hadn't really thought about that.

That means I won't be able to tell señora Mimí the best parts of my day or the things I'd do over, the way I usually do on our walks home.

We won't stop in Mr. Ruiz's shop to buy peanuts to feed our squirrels.

And I won't get to open her lobby
mailbox with the little silver key.

Or press the top elevator button
and race Pancho to the door.

By the time we get to señora Mimí's apartment, nothing
makes me feel better. Not even buttered crackers.

So I find a blanket and curl up with Pancho under
the kitchen table.

"No more señora Mimí," I whisper to Pancho.
I'm sure I see his ears droop.

After a long while, señora Mimí comes to find us.

"Abuela is coming tonight," I say. All at once, the words don't taste like candy anymore.

Señora Mimí crawls underneath to sit beside me. Then she says, "Grandmothers love us in a very special way, so I know you are excited about your abuela. But I will miss you, Ana, and I feel a little sad."

I toss the blanket aside and crawl into her lap.
I hold her braid above my lip like a mustache
until she laughs.

"I am so glad we'll still be neighbors," she says.
"Will you promise to visit me?"

"Abuela and I can come every day for a snack," I say.
"You'll have to buy more crackers, though. Pancho eats
so many."

"A wonderful idea! That way, we can all become good friends!"

While Nelson naps, we decide to draw pictures for
Abuela's room of the things we will do together.
It keeps us busy until Mami comes to get me.

"Ready?" Mami asks.

I give señora Mimí a kiss on each cheek and gather my things.

"See you next week," I tell her.

"Next week and always," she says. "I'll be here."

I can't wait to tell Abuela all about señora Mimí.